P9-CEX-502

The
Middle Sister

By MIRIAM E. MASON

Illustrated by WAYNE BLICKENSTAFF

SCHOLASTIC SBS BOOK SERVICES

Published by Scholastic Book Services, a division
of Scholastic Magazines, Inc., New York, N.Y.

Copyright © 1947 by The Macmillan Company. Copyright © 1963 by Scholastic Magazines, Inc. This edition is published by Scholastic Book Services, a division of Scholastic Magazines, Inc., by arrangement with The Macmillan Company.

4th printing . . . . November 1966

Printed in the U.S.A.

CONTENTS

THE MIDDLE SISTER

The Apple Hill 7
Uncle Romeo and the Lion's Tooth 14
The Secret Bargain 19
The Brave Thought 23

MISS APPLESEED

Father's Big Surprise 27
Sarah Samantha's Treasure 30
At the Sale 35
The Traveling Tree 42

THE HOMESTEAD

A Place for the Tree 45
The Hunt 50
The Homesick Tree 55
The Long Winter 61
The Singing Tree 67
Counting 72

GRASSHOPPER SUMMER

The Strange-looking Cloud 77

Sarah Samantha on Guard 83

HARVEST TIME

The Baker's Dozen 89

Mrs. Rollvag and the Apples 92

The Moonlight Race 99

Sarah Samantha's Indian 107

Little Buffalo 114

THE APPLE DUMPLING

The Great Day 121

Sugar 'n' Spice 128

And Then There Was One 132

The Present 137

The Lion's Tooth 140

The Charm That Worked 143

THE MIDDLE SISTER

The Apple Hill

"WE MUST MAKE an apple dumpling for supper tonight," said Mrs. Glossbrenner to her three daughters one bright day in the early springtime.

Uncle Romeo was coming for supper. He was the Glossbrenners' favorite uncle, and they always had a fine meal when he came.

Everybody in the family wanted to help get ready for Uncle Romeo. There were two big boys in the family, and they had gone down to the river to catch fish for Uncle Romeo, because Uncle Romeo liked fish.

Mr. Glossbrenner had gone to the mill to have some corn made into fresh corn meal. Uncle Romeo loved corn bread.

"I will sweep and dust the spare room, where Uncle Romeo will sleep tonight," said Miney. She was the oldest of Mrs. Glossbrenner's three daughters. She was almost eleven.

"I will bake some cakes and pies," said Mrs. Glossbrenner. "I will boil some ham and fry some chickens and sausages."

This was a good many years ago, when people had very large company dinners, with as many kinds of food as they could think of set on the table.

"What can I do?" asked Sarah Samantha, the middle sister, who was just eight.

"You may go out to the apple hill and get the apples for the dumplings," answered her mother.

In those days country people dug deep holes in the ground for their apples, potatoes, cabbages, and turnips. When the holes were covered with straw and were piled high with earth, the food stayed good all winter.

Sarah Samantha took the basket and went out toward the apple hill. She did not mind going after the apples, but she wished she did not need to go alone. She wished that Miney would come downstairs and help get the apples out of the hill. Miney was brave. She was not afraid of the ducks, the pigs, the bees in their hives, or anything.

"I will soon be ready for the apples!" called her mother.

Sarah Samantha walked slowly, looking about in a timid way.

The ducks out by the garden quacked and came running as she went by with her basket. They were big, greedy ducks with large beaks and hoarse voices. Eating interested them more than anything else in the world.

When Sarah Samantha did not throw any corn out of the basket, they were disappointed. Some of the biggest ones nibbled at her legs with their long beaks.

"I am not afraid of you!" said Sarah Samantha, running from the ducks. "I am not very much afraid of you!"

Her big sister Miney would have waved the basket and said "Get out!" and the ducks would have run from Miney. But Sarah Samantha was not so old or so big or so brave as Miney, so the ducks ran after her with loud quacks.

She ran fast through the back yard and through the garden gate. Then she sat down on an old woodpile to rest.

Suddenly she happened to look down at the other end of the woodpile. An old gray rat was sitting there looking at her. He was an old, old grandfather rat with hardly any whiskers or teeth, and he wouldn't have bothered to run after Sarah Samantha for anything.

"I am not afraid of you — not very much afraid," said Sarah Samantha, getting up quickly. "But I just don't like your looks!"

She hurried faster out to the apple hill. But when she got there, she stopped very quickly.

A pig was standing by the apple hill. It could smell the good smell of apples, and it had been trying and trying to reach the apples with its nose.

"Get out!" said Sarah Samantha, trying to sound like Miney. But her voice was very small and soft, and the pig was not frightened. "Go away!" said Sarah Samantha, almost in a whisper.

The pig was pleased. It made a noise like "Goody, goody, goody!" It supposed that Sarah Samantha was going to get some of the good-smelling apples for it.

It came closer to Sarah Samantha, making a sound like "Goody, goody, goody" and sniffing at the basket with its cold, wet nose.

"Go away!" said Sarah Samantha.

She turned around and ran as fast as she could. Although she had never told anybody, she was really afraid of pigs. They had such hungry ways and unpleasant voices. Some pigs had bad tempers, too. A bad-tempered mother pig had once chased Sarah Samantha.

Sarah Samantha climbed on the wagon in the barnyard and sat there. "If I wait here long enough, maybe that pig will go away from the apple hill," she thought.

She sat on the wagon a good while, but the pig did not go away. It stayed by the apple hill, sniffing and digging with its nose.

"Perhaps if I would take some corn to the pig, it would go away from the hill," thought Sarah Samantha at last.

The corn was in the corncrib behind the barn. When Sarah Samantha went out there, she saw the old ram walking around the corncrib, looking cross and hungry.

A ram is a father sheep. Mr. Glossbrenner's ram was rather old and cross, but he liked to play jokes on people. His favorite joke was to run up behind people and bump them with his head.

When he saw Sarah Samantha, he came running over with a cross look on his face, ready to bump her.

"Oh, dear!" said Sarah Samantha, hurrying back into the house with her empty basket.

Her mother was waiting, with the dumpling dough rolled out and ready on the table.

"Here you are at last!" she said. "If we do not hurry, we will not get the dumpling ready in time for Uncle Romeo's supper!" Then she saw that the basket was empty. "Where are the apples?" she asked.

Sarah Samantha hung her head. "The ducks ran after me," she said. "A rat looked at me. The old pig stood at the apple hill and grunted. The old ram chased me with his head. So I came back to the house!"

Mrs. Glossbrenner looked disappointed. "And now Uncle Romeo will not have his apple dumpling for supper!" she scolded. "Because of some ducks and a rat and a pig and a ram, poor Uncle Romeo must go without apple dumpling!"

Sarah Samantha hung her head. She was a timid little girl, and she never talked back to her mother.

Uncle Romeo and the Lion's Tooth

JUST AT SUPPERTIME, Uncle Romeo came driving up to the front gate. Everybody ran out to meet him.

The boys took his fine buggy and horse out to the barnyard, where they could feed the horse. Uncle Romeo's buggy had bright-red wheels, and his horse took high steps and tossed its head when it walked. The boys were proud to have such a horse and buggy in the barnyard.

Uncle Romeo carried Annie, the youngest, on his shoulder. Miney walked on one side, and Sarah Samantha walked on the other side. Mr. Glossbrenner hurried ahead to open the door, and Mrs. Glossbrenner came behind to close it.

The kitchen was filled with delicious smells.

The table was set with the best dishes, and the pink lamp was already lighted.

Uncle Romeo stopped and looked all around the kitchen. He closed his eyes and took a deep breath. A happy smile came on his handsome face. His black whiskers shook with happiness.

"What a wonderful supper I see!" said Uncle Romeo. He took some more deep breaths. "What a wonderful supper I smell!" he cried. "All my favorite foods!"

The Glossbrenners smiled, because they were

glad to have such a good supper for Uncle Romeo. Only Sarah Samantha did not smile very much. She was thinking about the apple dumpling which Uncle Romeo would not have.

Uncle Romeo always wore handsome clothes. He had on a fine black and white suit today with a green silk vest. Across the front of the vest hung his beautiful gold watch chain.

One end of the chain was fastened to Uncle Romeo's big gold watch. There was a special pocket in his vest for the watch. The boys often asked the time of day just so they could look at Uncle Romeo's gold watch.

On the other end of the chain was something even more interesting than a gold watch. It was a great, great big tooth. It was a lion's tooth and had once belonged to a real live lion named His Majesty.

His Majesty was a lion in the circus for which Uncle Romeo worked. He was a very large lion, with a big mouth and many teeth. When one of his teeth began to ache, and he did not want it any more, he allowed Uncle Romeo to have it.

"A lion's tooth is one of the finest watch charms in the world," Uncle Romeo often said.

He had brushed and polished the big white tooth till it shone like a looking glass and was much finer-looking than when His Majesty had it.

Uncle Romeo had a special job in the circus. It was a very important job. When spring came, Uncle Romeo would drive around in his buggy with big bright pictures of the circus. He would paste these bills on barns and fences so people would know about the circus.

These bills were very exciting to look at. They showed fierce lions, tigers, and elephants. Sarah Samantha always felt like shivering when she looked at the pictures, because the animals looked so dangerous.

But she liked to look at the pictures anyway, and she liked to hear Uncle Romeo tell of his exciting adventures in the circus.

All the family listened as Uncle Romeo talked. They almost forgot to eat, because they were so interested.

At last it was time for dessert. Mrs. Glossbrenner brought on the cakes, the pies, the pickled peaches, and the preserved crab apples.

"But where is Uncle Romeo's apple dumpling?" asked Miney, who was helping to bring the dessert.

Mrs. Glossbrenner looked all around. "Dear me, yes, where *is* the apple dumpling?" she asked. "Something must have happened to it!"

"Never mind," said Uncle Romeo kindly. "I can get along very well with what we have."

Uncle Romeo ate four pieces of pie, two pieces of cake, and a good many pickled peaches and crab-apple preserves.

But Sarah Samantha hung her head and felt ashamed. "A brave man like Uncle Romeo deserves an apple dumpling!" she thought sadly.

The Secret Bargain

"SHALL WE go out and look at Miss Apple-seed?" Uncle Romeo asked Sarah Samantha the next morning.

Miss Appleseed was a small apple tree which grew out in the back yard between a very old rosebush and a very tall cherry tree. She belonged to Sarah Samantha. Uncle Romeo had brought her for a birthday present when Sarah Samantha was three years old.

Uncle Romeo and Sarah Samantha went out to see if the apple tree was growing. Miss Appleseed did not grow fast, and never had any apples. But Uncle Romeo and Sarah Samantha loved her just the same.

The ducks and the old mother pig came running up to Uncle Romeo, and the old ram tried to come up behind and play his joke. Sarah Samantha hung tight to her uncle's hand and felt quite brave.

"You are not afraid of anything, are you?" she asked Uncle Romeo.

The handsome man smiled. "A person who wears a lion's tooth for a charm should be as brave as a lion," he answered.

Then Sarah Samantha said, "I have a great favor to ask of you. It is a very important favor."

"What is the favor?" asked Uncle Romeo kindly.

Sarah Samantha told him her greatest wish. "I would like to have a lion's tooth like yours. I would wear it around my neck, and I would be very brave. Do you suppose His Majesty has another tooth he can spare?"

Uncle Romeo thought for a minute. Then he said, "I am afraid His Majesty needs the rest of his teeth. But I will make a bargain with you. It will be a secret bargain."

Sarah Samantha listened and waited.

"You know how I love apple dumplings," said Uncle Romeo. "I will make a bargain with you for an apple dumpling. If you will make me an apple dumpling all by yourself from apples picked from Miss Appleseed, I will give you my lion's tooth."

"For my very own?" whispered Sarah Samantha.

Uncle Romeo nodded his head. "I would not sell my lion's tooth for money, but you know how I love apple dumplings. For years I have wished for apple dumplings made of apples which grew on Miss Appleseed."

Sarah Samantha and Uncle Romeo made their bargain.

At last Uncle Romeo drove off in his fine buggy with the red wheels. His high-stepping horse tossed its head and ran down the road very fast.

"Good-by, good-by, good-by!" called the Glossbrenners, waving their hands.

Uncle Romeo waved back. "Don't forget our bargain!" he called to Sarah Samantha.

Sarah Samantha went back to the house to help wash the breakfast dishes. She did not feel quite so sad now because of the apple dumpling.

"Just wait till I make my apple dumpling for Uncle Romeo," she thought. "It will be as big as a dishpan. And when I have my lion's tooth, I will not be afraid of anything!"

She looked out the kitchen window and saw the old ram, walking back and forth in the barnyard, waiting to play his joke on somebody.

"*You* wait till I get my lion's tooth," she called to the old ram. She felt braver already.

The Brave Thought

SEVERAL DAYS passed by. Sarah Samantha thought often of her bargain with Uncle Romeo. It was a pleasant thought.

"How surprised everybody will be when I get my lion's tooth!" she thought. "I will be the bravest person in the family, and even the old ram cannot scare me when I have my lion's tooth!"

Every week Mrs. Glossbrenner took her butter and eggs to town. She traded them at the store for money or things which the family needed.

One morning she was getting ready for her trip to town. She was putting eggs into a big basket.

"I need five more eggs," she said. "If I have five more eggs, I will have fourteen dozen eggs to take to the store."

She sent Sarah Samantha out to the chicken house to hunt five more eggs.

Sarah Samantha went to the chicken house and looked in all the nests. The eggs had already been gathered that day, and the hens had not had time to lay more.

There was one nest from which the eggs had not been gathered. The black hen was on the nest, hiding the eggs under her warm feathers. She wanted to keep on sitting there until the eggs hatched into little chickens.

She made a scolding, cross noise when Sarah Samantha came up to the nest. She was a good-tempered hen most of the time, but she did not want to be bothered now.

Sarah Samantha knew there were several eggs in the nest, and they were nice fresh eggs which the other hens had laid that morning. She tried to push the hen away with her hand, but the hen scolded harder and would not move.

Then she reached under the warm feathers to get the eggs. The hen pecked her hand very hard. Every time Sarah Samantha took out an egg, the hen pecked her hand. Tears came into Sarah Samantha's eyes and ran down her cheeks.

Her brother Robert looked in. He saw the cross old hen, and Sarah Samantha standing there with tears in her eyes. He came into the chicken house laughing.

"Don't be scared of an old setting hen!" he said.

He lifted the black hen from the nest and tossed her to the floor, paying no attention to her scoldings and flappings.

Sarah Samantha took the eggs and went into the house. There were three little red marks on her hand where the hen had pecked her.

"Just wait till I get my lion's tooth," she thought. "Then I will not be afraid of an old setting hen, either!"

Such brave thoughts made her feel better, and the red places on her hand soon stopped hurting.

MISS APPLESEED

Father's Big Surprise

NEARLY EVERY DAY Sarah Samantha ran out
and looked closely at Miss Appleseed. She
looked over each branch and twig, hunting for
apple blossoms which would grow into apples.

One day she found several buds. "If each of
these buds makes one apple, I can make a

large apple dumpling for Uncle Romeo," she thought, feeling very happy.

"How cheerful you look!" said her father to Sarah Samantha as they sat at dinner that day.

All the family looked at the middle sister. There was a bright smile on her face, as if she might be thinking of Christmas or a picnic.

"I have a secret!" said Sarah Samantha. "It is a cheerful secret!"

"I have a secret, too!" said Mr. Glossbrenner. "I have a fine surprise for all of you!"

"Tell us now!" begged the two big boys and the three little girls. They were all wondering what their father's surprise could be.

So Mr. Glossbrenner told them his surprise. "We are going to move away from here," he said. "I have traded this tiny little farm in Ohio for a fine large homestead in Minnesota!"

"What is a homestead, Father?" asked Miney, and Silas asked, "Where is Minnesota, Father?"

Mr. Glossbrenner answered proudly, "Minnesota is a fine large, rich new state many hundred miles from here."

Mrs. Glossbrenner said in a brave way, "A homestead is a grand big farm, in the new state, where you will have many acres around your home instead of a few acres."

"When shall we move, Father?" asked Sarah Samantha in a wee, small voice.

Her father spoke cheerfully, "We shall move as soon as we have a sale and can get packed. The homestead is waiting for us. That is the nice part of the surprise! We can go in two or three weeks!"

Mr. Glossbrenner looked up and down the table, smiling proudly at each of his five children. He was delighted because he had given them such a big surprise.

"Just think," he said. "In a few weeks we will be miles and miles away from here, living on our own homestead in the grand new state of Minnesota!"

Sarah Samantha's Treasure

Most of the Glossbrenner children were pleased because they were going to Minnesota. None of them had ever traveled very far.

"Just think how exciting it will be to go way out to Minnesota!" said Miney every day.

"It will be grand to have a great, great big farm with many acres, instead of this small farm!" the boys and their father said over and over.

Sarah Samantha was the only one of the

children who did not want to go away. She did not feel pleased about the long journey or the big homestead.

When the other children asked over and over, "How soon can we start?" Sarah Samantha hung her head and looked sad.

She knew that they would have to leave many things behind them when they went to Minnesota. There would not be room in the new house for all the furniture. There would not be room in the new barn for all the animals. The freight car was not big enough to hold everything.

"I will have to leave Miss Appleseed, and I will never get to pick her apples and make them into a dumpling which I can trade to Uncle Romeo for a lion's tooth!" thought Sarah Samantha, feeling very sad.

But one day her father said something which made them all feel cheerful.

"Next week will be our sale," he said, "but we will not sell everything. I want each of you to choose one special treasure to take along."

"I choose the melodeon," said Miney at once.

The melodeon was the little organ which stood in the parlor.

"I choose the black colt!" said Robert quickly.

All chose, one by one, what they liked best. It was like the game of London Bridge.

"What do you choose, Sarah Samantha?" asked Mr. Glossbrenner at last.

"I choose Miss Appleseed," said Sarah Samantha firmly.

All the family looked at her in surprise. None of them thought she had made a good choice. All of them told her other things which would be a greater treasure to her.

"Miss Appleseed is my greatest treasure," said Sarah Samantha, as if she really meant it.

Silas looked disgusted. "Who ever heard of taking a little old apple tree all the way to Minnesota?" he said.

Robert looked disgusted, too. "That apple tree never has any apples on it. It would be better to take some apples from the apple hill."

Mr. Glossbrenner thought for a minute. "That is a long journey for an apple tree which is not very strong anyway," he said. "I am not sure the tree would live."

"I still choose Miss Appleseed!" said Sarah Samantha. "You promised, Father. You promised we could choose our own treasure."

"Of course," said Mr. Glossbrenner. "And a promise is a promise. We will take your apple tree to Minnesota with us."

"Don't blame anybody if the apple tree dies and you have no treasure!" said Miney in her most bossy voice.

"Miss Appleseed won't die!" cried Sarah Samantha happily. "I can hardly wait to see her growing on the homestead!"

Sarah Samantha ran out the back door and down through the garden to where the small apple tree stood between the tall cherry tree and the old rosebush.

She was so excited that she hardly noticed

the ducks running after her and quacking for food.

"You are going to Minnesota with us," she whispered to Miss Appleseed as she looked over the branches hunting for more buds which would grow into apples.

"How silly to take along a good-for-nothing apple tree which never has any apples!" said Robert.

"Sarah Samantha has a right to her tree if she wants it," said Mrs. Glossbrenner. But she shook her head in a puzzled way. "I never knew that Sarah Samantha was such a stubborn child!" she said.

At the Sale

THE DAY OF THE SALE was bright and beautiful. "What a fine day for a sale!" thought everybody when they looked out at the weather.

The Glossbrenner family had been very busy getting ready for the sale. They had to look at all their things and decide which to take and which to sell.

One room in the house was piled full of furniture and things which would go along to Minnesota. The front yard was filled with things which were for sale.

People began coming early in the morning. First came the ladies of the church who were going to cook dinner and sell it to the people at the sale. In that way the ladies would earn lots of money to buy new carpet for the church.

Whole families came driving up in their wagons and carriages. Then men wanted to look at Father's pigs and cows. The ladies would see about buying some of the furniture. The children would play and have a good time. It was just like a big picnic.

The auctioneer was a man with a very loud voice who sold the things. He had a special way of selling the things. He would stand in front of the crowd and talk about the things which were for sale.

"What am I offered for this fine pig?" he would cry out, if he were selling a pig.

He would talk about the fine pig and try to get the people to pay lots of money for it. The person who offered the most money would get the pig.

Most people had looked over all the things and decided what they wished to buy. Several ladies had looked at Mother's big corner cupboard and decided to buy it. Several men had made up their minds to buy the old ram.

Mrs. Perkins had walked all around the house and the barnyard, deciding what she wished to buy. Mrs. Perkins was a large, fat lady with a stern manner and a voice almost as loud as the auctioneer's voice.

She could not hear very well, and it was hard to talk to her.

Mrs. Perkins looked around a long time before she found anything she wished to buy. Her house was already full of furniture, and her barnyard was already crowded with animals.

At last she saw something she wanted. It was Sarah Samantha's quilted petticoat, and it was hanging on the clothesline in the back yard.

The petticoat was not for sale. Mother had washed all the best clothes and hung them out to dry yesterday. The petticoat was thick and it was still a little damp.

Sarah Samantha had forgotten to bring in her quilted petticoat before the sale began. So when Mrs. Perkins saw it hanging from the line, her black eyes sparkled.

"This is just what I need to make cushions for my rocking chair!" she said in her loud voice. She unpinned the quilted petticoat. "I will ask the auctioneer to sell this right away!" she said, carrying the petticoat around to the front yard.

Sarah Samantha ran after her. "The petticoat is not for sale, please!" she said.

Mrs. Perkins did not hear very well, and Sarah Samantha spoke in a small voice.

"Yes, yes, yes!" cried Mrs. Perkins in her loud voice. "It is a fine day for a sale, child, but I am in a hurry. I must go as soon as I buy this petticoat."

"But it is my petticoat. I do not want to sell it!" said Sarah Samantha, feeling rather afraid of Mrs. Perkins' sharp eyes and loud voice.

"Yes, yes, yes!" roared Mrs. Perkins. "It is a nice petticoat. It will make fine cushions for my rocking chair!"

She hurried over to the auctioneer and gave him Sarah Samantha's quilted petticoat with the pink roses on it.

"Sell this right away," she told the auctioneer. "I want to buy it."

She was a very large lady with a very loud voice, and the auctioneer at once did as she told him to.

"What am I offered for this beautiful garment?" he called, holding up the petticoat for all the people to see.

"I offer twenty-five cents!" answered Mrs. Perkins in her loudest voice.

She looked over the crowd in a stern way. Nobody else offered anything for the petticoat.

Mrs. Perkins took Sarah Samantha's petticoat and paid a quarter for it. She hurried away with the petticoat over her arm.

"Why did you sell your best petticoat?" whispered Miney to Sarah Samantha. "Now when you get dressed in your best clothes for our trip to Minnesota, you will not have a quilted petticoat."

Tears ran down Sarah Samantha's cheeks. "I did not want to sell the petticoat!" she said. "But Mrs. Perkins wanted to buy it. She is so big and her voice is so loud, and she held onto the petticoat!"

"I would have taken it away from her!" said Miney, tossing her head. "I would have taken it out of her hands. I am not afraid of her big voice or her sharp black eyes or her deaf ears."

"You are so brave, Miney!" said Sarah Samantha. A few more tears ran down her cheeks, but she wiped them away.

"Some day I will be brave, too!" she thought. "Just wait till I get my lion's tooth. Then I will not be afraid of Mrs. Perkins, no matter how much she wants to buy my quilted petticoat!"

The Traveling Tree

A T LAST the day came for traveling. Miney's melodeon had been packed in a box and loaded onto a wagon with other things. All the things would be taken to town and put into a railroad car for the long ride to Minnesota.

The black colt had already been taken to town to wait for the train.

Last of all, Father got Miss Appleseed ready for her trip. He had to be very careful.

"Traveling is not easy for an apple tree this time of year," he said.

There was a special way of getting the tree ready. First, Father dug carefully all about the roots of the little tree so he would not break any of them. Then he dipped the roots in a puddle of mud, over and over until Miss Appleseed's roots were covered in a ball of mud. After that he packed straw all around the damp mud ball.

"This will help to keep the roots from getting too dry," he said.

Then he found an old horse blanket. He wrapped the old blanket all around the straw-covered ball and sewed it on good and tight. Finally he dipped the roots in water once more.

"Now Miss Appleseed is dressed up and ready to go," he told Sarah Samantha. "It is a long trip, but I think she will be all right."

Sarah Samantha watched them load up the railroad car. The black colt and the cows did not want to get in and had to be coaxed. It was hard work to get the melodeon and the black iron kitchen stove through the door.

Last of all came the little apple tree, all dressed up in mud and straw and the old horse blanket. Father put it carefully in a place where it would not be crushed or lost.

When all the things were loaded, the family climbed onto the passenger car in front of the freight cars.

The bell rang and the train whistled. Several people had come to say good-by to the Glossbrenner family. They waved and called as the train began to move.

At last they were really started. The town was far behind. The fields and the farms had a strange look.

The train whistled now and then. It was a wild, lonely sound. It made Sarah Samantha think of far-off places.

"The homestead will seem more like home with Miss Appleseed there," she thought.

THE HOMESTEAD

A Place for the Tree

THE JOURNEY on the train seemed very long and tiresome. All the Glossbrenners were glad when the conductor went through the cars shouting, "Deerhorn! Deerhorn!"

Deerhorn was the name of the town in Minnesota where the family would get off.

"Deerhorn is one of the finest and fastest-growing towns in Minnesota," Mr. Glossbrenner had told his family.

The children crowded to the doorway of the train, anxious to see the new town.

Deerhorn was a very small town. It had one long street with some stores and a blacksmith shop on it. Behind the long street were several houses.

"Shall we live in one of these houses, Father?" asked Miney, looking up and down.

"Oh my, no!" answered Mr. Glossbrenner. "We will live on a fine large homestead with acres and acres of ground around it. The homestead is a few miles out in the country."

Mr. Glossbrenner and his family walked down the street until they came to a large barn. There was a sign above the barn which said LIVERY STABLE.

"Here we can hire some horses and wagons to take us to our new home," said the father.

He hired a small wagon with two horses to take his family out to the homestead. Then he hired a large wagon with four horses to bring the furniture and things.

The black colt and the cows were tied to the back of the furniture wagon. They did not mind the long walk because they were tired of standing still.

Mr. Glossbrenner sat on the seat of the small wagon and drove the horses. A man from the livery stable came behind with the furniture.

As they drove along, Mr. Glossbrenner admired the fine country.

"Just see how big the farms are!" he told his wife and children. "Here we will not be crowded by neighbors. Here we shall have all the room we want!"

"Oh my, yes!" said Mrs. Glossbrenner in a brave voice. "Nobody could want more room than we shall have here!"

"The roads are not crowded, either!" said

Robert, looking up and down to see if there were any other wagons on the road.

Nobody was in sight.

"It is such a new-looking country!" said Miney, trying to see some other houses along the rough road. "Why, even the roads are new-looking!"

"We are going to like it here!" smiled Mr. Glossbrenner. "Just think! We have a house all ready for us on our homestead!"

After traveling for a long time, they came to a very small house with very large fields all around it. Behind the house was a barn, and behind the fields were tall trees.

"How little and scared that house looks with all those big empty fields around it!" said Sarah Samantha.

But her father did not hear her. He was stopping the horses. There was a proud smile on his face.

"This is our homestead!" he said happily. "Welcome to your new home, children!"

The Hunt

"HERE COMES the wagon!" cried Silas, who had been watching and watching.

Now the family could see the four horses pulling the big loaded wagon. The colt and the cows were coming along behind.

"I can hardly wait to see how things look in the new house!" cried Miney.

Sarah Samantha cried, "I can hardly wait to see Miss Appleseed growing outside my window!"

The big wagon drove into the yard. Robert hurried to lead the black colt away to his new barn. Silas untied his pet cow and took her to the barn, too.

The drivers helped to unload the things from the wagon. They lifted out the black stove and put it in the kitchen. They set

Miney's melodeon in its place. They helped put the beds together.

"It seems more like home every minute!" said Mrs. Glossbrenner happily.

Sarah Samantha kept watching and waiting for Miss Appleseed.

"Surely Miss Appleseed will come next," she kept thinking as things were lifted out of the wagon.

But at last there was nothing left in the big wagon. And still Miss Appleseed had not been taken out.

"Where is my apple tree?" asked Sarah Samantha. "Have you forgotten it?"

The drivers scratched their heads and looked at one another.

"The apple tree was on when we started," said the red-haired driver. "I remember it well."

"We put it in the wagon last of all," said the gray-haired driver. "The wagon was full. I set the tree on top of the barrel of dishes!"

"But it is gone now!" said Sarah Samantha. She felt like crying, but there was no time for crying now. "You have lost my apple tree!" she said in a stern voice.

The drivers nodded their heads. "The road is rough. The tree must have fallen off along the way."

"We must go back and get the tree — at once!" said Sarah Samantha. She stood very straight. She tried to sound like Mrs. Perkins.

"It is a long trip back to Deerhorn," said the gray-haired driver. "We thought we would stay here all night and start back early in the morning. Our horses are tired."

"We may find the tree on our way back," said the red-haired driver. "Not many people travel that road."

"We must find the tree tonight," said Sarah Samantha. "Tomorrow might be too late!"

"You are so stubborn, Sarah Samantha!" scolded Robert. "But you cannot go by yourself to hunt the apple tree. I will go with you. We will ride the colt."

Robert brought the black colt from his new place in the barn. He got on the colt's back, and Sarah Samantha got on behind him. They rode off to hunt the lost apple tree.

"This is lots of trouble," scolded Robert, who was really enjoying the ride. "It is dangerous, too. We might meet some wild animals or even some Indians, or we might even get lost on the prairie."

"I do hope we find the tree before it gets too dark," said Sarah Samantha, looking in all directions. "It would be hard to see a little apple tree in the dark on this strange road."

"We may ride all night and still not find that tree," said her brother in a gloomy voice.

But they had not gone more than three miles before they saw Miss Appleseed lying in the road. There was a very rough place in the road, and the tree had jolted off the wagon.

"It is a good thing we came back," said Sarah Samantha as they were going home with the tree. "Suppose some wagons had come along and run over Miss Appleseed!"

It was almost dark when they got back to the homestead. The prairie seemed very large and lonely. Strange animals called in loud voices. The house looked small. Sarah Samantha felt a little frightened.

"It is a good thing I have my apple tree," she thought. "I am going to need a lion's tooth out here. When I get my lion's tooth, I will not be afraid to go riding on the black colt. I will not be afraid of the night, or the strange noises, or the bigness of our homestead!"

It was a brave thought and made her feel better.

The Homesick Tree

THE NEXT MORNING Mr. Glossbrenner planted the apple tree in the place Sarah Samantha had chosen.

He dug a deep hole for Miss Appleseed's roots. Sarah Samantha took off the old horse blanket and the straw. She helped to put the tree in place and cover up the roots.

She brought a bucket of water and poured it on the tree.

"Now you are at home," she said to Miss Appleseed.

Every day she hunted for buds on the little tree and hoped to see green apples growing. She was pleased to notice leaves on the tree.

But after a few days the apple tree did not seem so well. No more buds came. The leaves did not grow bigger. Some of them dried up and soon fell off.

"I do wonder what is the matter with Miss

Appleseed," thought Sarah Samantha when she looked out at the tree.

"Perhaps the tree is thirsty," said Mrs. Glossbrenner.

The days were getting warm now, and the weather was dry.

Sarah Samantha thought of the brook back in Ohio. She wished she might see the brook again and go wading in it.

"I do wish we had a nice brook on our homestead," she said to Miney as she helped her wash the dishes one warm day. "It would be fun to go wading in the brook. The water feels so comfortable to your bare feet!"

"Here we have a river!" said Miney proudly as she scrubbed a big skillet. "A river is bigger than a brook. And a homestead is bigger than a farm!"

"Sometimes I get tired of so much bigness!" said Sarah Samantha as she looked out the door.

As far as she could see, there was only the homestead.

"You may have the dishwater for your apple tree," Miney told her sister as they finished the dishes.

People on a homestead did not waste water. Water was scarce and had to be carried to the house. Water which had been used for washing dishes or taking a bath was still useful.

Sarah Samantha carried the pan of dishwater out and poured it around the roots of the apple tree. The water was soapy and looked dull.

"I would not like a drink of soapy dishwater no matter how thirsty I felt," thought Sarah Samantha. It seemed to her that Miss Appleseed looked smaller and more dried up than she did yesterday. "I think you are homesick!" said Sarah Samantha to the little tree. "The homestead is so big and so strange, and dishwater has such a disagreeable taste."

She wondered how to keep Miss Appleseed from being homesick. At last she decided to bring fresh water from the river for the tree to drink.

"Annie can walk along with me for company," she thought. "It will be a nice little walk for both of us."

Little Annie was glad to go with Sarah Samantha to get water. She had to walk slowly, and she sometimes fell down, for she was a very small girl.

But she talked and laughed and was cheerful. She listened and laughed when Sarah Samantha told her interesting stories about brave people.

Sometimes gophers came out of their holes and looked at the girls walking toward the river. Gophers are animals which live in holes in the ground in the prairie country.

The gophers had sharp faces with small bright eyes and very long front teeth. They looked like big rats, Sarah Samantha thought. She always felt like running when she saw a gopher looking out at her from his hole.

But of course she could not run away from Annie, who poked along on her fat little legs.

She could not run with a bucket of water in her hand.

So she had to walk slowly past the gopher holes and pretend that she was not afraid of gophers or snakes, or any of the wild creatures around the homestead.

"Some day, when I have my lion's tooth, I am going to walk up to a gopher hole and look right in at the gopher. How scared he will be to see my eyes staring at him!"

But even with all the buckets of water, Miss Appleseed still seemed a little homesick. One time when Sarah Samantha was pouring the water on the tree's roots she saw some tiny toothmarks on the bark of the tree.

She told her father about this, and he thought awhile. Then he made a little fence all around Miss Appleseed. It was made of tiny poles pounded into the ground. They were so close together that nothing could get in between them.

"Now Miss Appleseed has a little picket

fence just like we had around our old home back in Ohio!" he said.

Sarah Samantha painted the small picket fence with whitewash, and it looked just beautiful.

Soon Miss Appleseed began to grow. New leaves and buds came on her branches. She grew taller.

"She is not homesick any more," thought Sarah Samantha happily. "With fresh water to drink and a picket fence around her, she feels at home."

The Long Winter

THE FIRST SUMMER on the homestead went by. Autumn came. The wild plum trees along the river were covered with bright-red plums.

But there were no apples on Sarah Samantha's apple tree.

"Wait until next year," her father told her. "A tree needs a year to grow in after it is moved."

"Miss Appleseed has been growing," said Mrs. Glossbrenner. "She is taller than when we lived back in Ohio."

"You children have been growing, too!" Mr. Glossbrenner told his children proudly. "Already the boys are taller than I am!"

They built a new room on the house.

"For such a fast-growing family, four rooms are not enough!" the father said.

One afternoon the children heard a great noise above them. They looked up into the sky. There went a great crowd of wild geese flying along together.

"Those geese know that winter is coming," said Silas. "They are going south, where it is warm."

"Geese are smart birds," said Robert. "I would be glad to go south for the winter. It will be cold in Minnesota this winter!"

The geese cried out in wild, lonely voices as they flew through the sky.

"I wonder if they will fly over our old home in Ohio," said Sarah Samantha to herself.

It gave her a lonely feeling to think of the pretty house back in Ohio with the white picket fence around the yard, and the brook and orchard behind the garden.

"But Miss Appleseed makes it seem more like home," she said to herself when she looked out her window and saw the little tree growing all by itself. "Miss Appleseed is just like a piece of Ohio away out here in Minnesota."

One day when the boys went out to milk the cows they saw snowflakes falling through the air.

"Winter has begun! It is snowing!" cried Robert when he came in with his milk pail.

The family could hardly believe this.

"Back in Ohio the corn is still out in the fields," said Mrs. Glossbrenner. "The pumpkins are still lying on the ground."

"Winter comes early in Minnesota," Silas told his mother.

Mr. Glossbrenner added, "It comes early and stays late. But winter is such a cozy time when you have a warm house and a good fire, isn't it?"

The snow piled higher and higher. The three sisters could hear it blowing against the roof and windows when they were tucked into bed.

"Snow is noisy out here in Minnesota," said Sarah Samantha, listening.

A few snowflakes blew in through a crack and fell on the sisters' faces.

"I am not afraid of the snow," said Miney. "We have a warm house and a cozy featherbed with heavy covers. Let it snow."

Sarah Samantha was good and warm. She slept in the middle because she was the middle sister. The featherbed was deep and soft, and the blankets were warm and thick.

"I do hope Miss Appleseed will not be too cold out there in the snow," she said to her sisters.

When the snow stopped falling, the weather was very cold. Mr. Glossbrenner and the boys piled straw and wild grass along the walls of the barn, and on the floor.

"Our animals are not used to such cold weather," said Mr. Glossbrenner. "They need extra covers to keep warm."

"Miss Appleseed is not used to such cold weather, either," said Sarah Samantha. "I think she needs some extra covers, too."

Sarah Samantha's brothers laughed at her. "Who ever heard of covering up an apple tree?" they teased. "Will you use your Sunday jacket or one of the best blankets?"

But Sarah Samantha paid no attention to their teasing. She scraped the snow away from Miss Appleseed. Then she brought wild grass from the barn and packed it inside the little picket fence.

She got the old horse blanket which Miss Appleseed had worn on her long journey. She put the old blanket over the tree's branches and tied it down tight.

"Now the apple tree looks like an old grandmother with a shawl tied over her head," the boys teased Sarah Samantha.

The middle sister did not mind their teasing. "Just wait until the apples are ripe!" she said.

The winter lasted a long, long time. The snow did not melt off all winter long. It got hard and icy, and new snow fell on top of it.

Often there were hard blizzards and storms. The wind howled and the snow blew against the windows.

Sarah Samantha did not mind the snow and the cold so much. She knew that Miss Appleseed was snug and warm under her covering.

As the winter went on, the snow piled higher and higher around the apple tree. Now Miss Appleseed looked like a little white hill outside the window.

"Here we have an apple hill right in the yard," said Sarah Samantha. "Isn't it home-like?"

The Singing Tree

ONE DAY a warm wind blew across the prairie. The snow grew very soft and wet. The drifts melted down. Spots of ground began to show at places in the whiteness.

Soon the snow was only spots of white here and there among the brown and green.

"What a fine winter we have had on our homestead!" Mr. Glossbrenner said happily each day. "And now spring is coming!"

"It makes me feel like singing," said Miney, who liked to sing.

One day Sarah Samantha went out and took the old horse blanket from Miss Appleseed. She pulled away the wild grass and straw from the tree's roots.

Under the old blanket and the damp straw the apple tree's branches were smooth and strong. Under the shining gray bark the limbs were green and full of sap.

"The apple tree has done well," Mr. Glossbrenner told his middle daughter. He showed her the many tiny little tight buds along the tree's branches. "These are fruit buds," he said. "They will turn into apple blossoms, and the blossoms will make the apples. I think we will have an apple crop this year!"

"I feel like singing," said Sarah Samantha. She thought to herself, "I do hope Uncle Romeo remembers our bargain."

A few days later Mr. Glossbrenner went to Deerhorn to do some trading. When he came home, he had a letter which had been at the post office.

The letter was from Uncle Romeo. It told about the circus, the weather in Ohio, and other interesting things. There was a special message for each one in the Glossbrenner family.

"Tell Sarah Samantha I have not forgotten

our bargain," wrote Uncle Romeo. "I still love apple dumplings better than any food in the world, and my lion's tooth is as sharp and white as ever!"

Sarah Samantha went out to see how the apple tree was growing. The buds were bigger, and some green leaves were beginning to uncurl.

"Miss Appleseed looks happy," thought Sarah Samantha. "I suppose she feels like singing, too!"

A week went by. One morning the three sisters waked early.

"I hear singing!" said Miney, sitting up in bed.

The window was open, and the sound came through the window. Annie climbed down from bed and ran to the window.

She looked out, and her blue eyes got round and big.

"The tree is singing!" she said.

Miney and Sarah Samantha looked out.

Sure enough, the singing came from the tree. It was a cheerful, gay sound.

Then Miney looked very sharply. "Birds have made a nest in the tree!" she said. "It is the birds who are singing!"

When the girls looked closely, they could see a nest down in the middle of the tree's branches. It was a very new nest. Two birds were just putting the last straws in it. They were happy and excited.

"How proud Miss Appleseed must feel!" cried Sarah Samantha. "She has never had a birds' nest of her own before!"

Back in Ohio the birds had always chosen the bigger trees. They had made nests in the cherry tree and in the old rosebush, but never in the small apple tree.

As days went by, the little mother bird sat quietly on her nest. One day the eggs hatched into noisy, cheerful, hungry young birds.

Apple blossoms covered the tree with pink and white flowers. Tiny little leaves were green among the blossoms.

The girls could hear the birds singing in the tree, but they could not see them. The bird family was cheerful and noisy. They sang most of the time.

It was easy for Sarah Samantha to imagine that the tree was singing. "Miss Appleseed must know what Uncle Romeo wrote to me in his letter," she thought as she listened to the music of the apple tree.

Counting

THE PETALS of the apple blossoms fell off. The blossoms turned into tiny little bits of apples no bigger than an appleseed. They were fuzzy little apples and they were a gray-green color.

"How many apples does it take to make an apple dumpling?" Sarah Samantha asked her mother.

Mrs. Glossbrenner answered, "That depends on whether the apples are large or small. It depends on whether the dumpling is big or little." She thought awhile. "Twelve middle-sized apples would make a nice middle-sized pan of middle-sized dumplings," she decided.

Sarah Samantha went out and counted the apples on her tree.

She had not learned to count past seventeen. When she came to seventeen she had to begin counting all over.

It took her a long time to count the apples because there were so many and they were so small.

Whenever she had counted seventeen apples, she had to begin counting again.

There were eleven times seventeen apples and three over. Sarah Samantha could not tell how many apples that was, but she knew it was enough for one apple dumpling.

She asked Miney, "How many apples are seventeen times eleven and three left over?"

Miney could count to a hundred, but she could not count seventeen times eleven.

When the boys came in, Miney asked Robert, "How many apples are seventeen times eleven with three left over?"

Robert got a paper and pencil and worked a long time. At last he had the answer.

"That would be a hundred and ninety apples!"

"I wonder how many apple dumplings you could make with a hundred and ninety apples!" wondered Sarah Samantha.

Robert could not answer such a hard problem. "We will ask Silas tonight," he said. "Silas is smart in numbers. Perhaps he can answer."

Silas and Mr. Glossbrenner had gone to Deerhorn that day.

When they came home, Robert asked his older brother, "If twelve medium-sized apples will make a dozen medium-sized apple dumplings, how many apple dumplings can you make with a hundred and ninety apples?"

Silas got his paper and pencil. He worked and figured a long time.

It was a hard problem, and the answer never came out the same.

"I am not sure whether the answer is five hundred dumplings or three and a half dumplings," he said, after thinking and working a long time.

Then Mr. and Mrs. Glossbrenner got pencils and paper and tried to figure the right number of apple dumplings. They got many different answers.

"I think the best way is just to wait until the apples are ripe and then count them," said Miney.

Just then there was a knock at the door. A man came in.

"I am your neighbor, Mr. MacDonald," he said. "I am going to start a school this summer for the children of the homesteads."

"Are you good at working hard problems in counting?" asked Mr. Glossbrenner.

Mr. MacDonald nodded his head. "Working hard problems is my favorite fun!" he answered.

"Here is a problem for you then," said Mrs. Glossbrenner. She told him the problem. "If it takes a dozen medium-sized apples to make twelve apple dumplings, how many dumplings can you make with a hundred and ninety apples?"

Mr. MacDonald smiled. "That is an easy problem," he said. "If twelve apples make a dozen dumplings, it takes one apple to make one dumpling. And a hundred and ninety apples would make a hundred and ninety dumplings!"

All the family admired Mr. MacDonald so much, they immediately promised that the four older children would come to his school.

"Homestead children must learn to count in large numbers," said Mr. Glossbrenner.

Sarah Samantha fell asleep dreaming of apple dumplings in long rows.

"It will take a big stove to bake a hundred and ninety apple dumplings!" she thought.

GRASSHOPPER SUMMER

The Strange-looking Cloud

SPRING turned into summer, and the tiny green apples grew round and shiny.

Mrs. Glossbrenner's garden grew fast, too. The corn in the cornfields was tall and healthy, with ears of corn beginning to show.

"This is going to be a good year for us," Mr. Glossbrenner said nearly every day. "That cold weather last winter was a good thing!"

Robert and Silas each had a cornfield. Miney had a small garden of her own near the big garden. Sarah Samantha had her apple tree. Even Annie had a little garden, in the front yard, with three onions, three cornstalks, and a potato in it.

"On a homestead there is room for everybody to have something," Mr. Glossbrenner said proudly as he looked over his fields.

Three days each week the Glossbrenner children went to Mr. MacDonald's school, where they were learning to work hard problems, write letters, and read long words.

One day when they were coming home, they heard a strange, roaring sound. The sky was blue and bright. The weather was clear.

"Surely it is not a storm!" said Robert, looking at the sky.

Silas pointed across the prairie. "What a strange-looking cloud!" he said. "It looks like a piece of black cloth in the sky!"

"It is coming lower and lower!" said Miney, looking.

"What a loud, roaring noise it makes!" shouted Robert. "Perhaps it is a cyclone!"

Sarah Samantha felt frightened. "Oh, dear! Oh, dear!" she cried. "I am so afraid of cyclones!"

She had never seen a cyclone, but she had heard about them. Cyclones are strong windstorms which blow down everything in their path.

"I don't want to blow away!" sobbed Sarah Samantha. "Let's run fast!"

Just then something bit her cheek. Sarah Samantha put up her hand. A big green grasshopper had jumped on her cheek and pinched it hard.

"Something bit my neck!" cried Miney. She brushed the back of her neck. "It is a nasty old green grasshopper!" she cried.

"Ouch! Ouch!" cried the boys together. "Something bit my leg!"

Two or three big hungry grasshoppers were on the boys' bare legs, taking bites.

The roaring became louder, and the strange black cloud fell lower and lower toward the earth.

The four children ran as fast as they could. Soon they came to their homestead. Their father and mother were outside the house looking around in an astonished way.

"What is happening?" screamed Miney.

Her mother screamed back, "It is grasshoppers. We must try to keep them off of the garden and cornfield!"

"I am afraid of grasshoppers!" sobbed Sarah Samantha. "They bite!"

The strange-looking cloud came lower. It changed from a cloud into many, many grasshoppers. The grasshoppers landed on the cornstalks and on the plants in the garden.

"We must fight them away!" cried Mr. Glossbrenner. "Come, boys!"

Mr. Glossbrenner and the boys hurried down to the river. They cut great armloads of willow branches.

Then the father and mother and four children went up and down the cornfields and the garden rows, waving the willow branches to frighten off the grasshoppers.

It was hard work. When the grasshoppers were not allowed to bite the cornstalks or the tomato plants, they bit the Glossbrenners.

Tears ran down Sarah Samantha's cheeks as she tried to scare off the grasshoppers. The grasshoppers were not easy to scare. They did not give up easily. Many of them jumped onto the willow branches and ate willow leaves in a hungry way.

"Work hard, children!" said Mr. Glossbrenner. "Do not be frightened by grasshoppers!"

Sarah Samantha on Guard

AT LAST the Glossbrenners were too tired to chase grasshoppers any longer. They went into the house and shut the door quickly, to keep out the grasshoppers.

Grasshoppers had bitten their faces and arms and legs. Grasshoppers had climbed into their hair. Annie looked at her family and began to cry.

"I shall go to bed and take a nap," said Sarah Samantha. "When I wake up, perhaps these grasshoppers will be gone."

She looked out the bedroom window. She saw something which made her forget how tired she was, and how hot and frightened.

Grasshoppers covered the apple tree. Grasshoppers were on every branch and every leaf.

Grasshoppers were chewing and chewing and chewing. Their sharp jaws bit into the green leaves and the tiny green apples. Their long back legs kept moving like fiddle bows. They made loud fiddle music as they chewed.

"How good! How good! How good!" they squeaked as they chewed.

Sarah Samantha felt very angry. "I will show those grasshoppers!" she said.

Her family looked at her in surprise.

"Where are you going, Sarah Samantha?" her parents asked in tired voices.

Sarah Samantha tied a dish towel over her head. She tied a scarf about her neck. She put on a pair of gloves.

"I am going to guard my apple tree!" she said.

Miney called as she went out the door, "Come back, come back, Sarah Samantha! There are too many grasshoppers. They will bite off your hair!"

"Come back, come back!" sobbed little Annie, who had never seen so many grasshoppers before.

But Sarah Samantha did not come back. She was very angry.

"You get out of here!" she screamed at the grasshoppers. "You leave Miss Appleseed alone!"

The grasshoppers paid no attention to Sarah Samantha. They loved the taste of the green apple leaves and the little green apples. They kept chewing and squeaking in a greedy, happy way.

But Sarah Samantha did not stop. She picked off the grasshoppers with her hands and killed each one with a stick of kindling wood. As fast as one was killed, another came. Some who could not get on Miss Appleseed hopped on Sarah Samantha. They bit through her calico dress, and through the dish towel around her head.

Every time a grasshopper bit her, Sarah Samantha grew more angry.

At last the grasshoppers got tired of trying and went away. The next morning the strange cloud was nowhere in sight. The loud roaring had stopped.

The homestead people went out and looked at their cornfields and gardens. It was a sad sight which they saw.

The grasshoppers had made a good feast before they went on. In many cornfields only the dry, empty stalks were left. The green blades and the little ears of corn had been eaten.

The tomatoes and the bean vines in the gardens were only dry little stalks.

Miss Appleseed had a battered look. She looked as if she had been in a hard fight. Most of the leaves had bites taken out of them. They looked like scraps of green lace. Most of the apples had been chewed. Many of them had been eaten.

But the apple tree was still alive and growing. There were a few green leaves left, and a few green apples.

Mr. Glossbrenner praised his middle daughter. "Not many girls would have been willing to stay out so long fighting the grasshoppers," he said.

"Not many girls would work so hard to save a little apple tree," praised Mrs. Glossbrenner.

"But Miss Appleseed is a very special apple tree," answered Sarah Samantha. "On a homestead like this it is important to have an apple tree!"

She thought to herself, "When I get my lion's tooth, I will not be afraid of those grasshoppers, no matter how hard they bite or how loud they roar!"

HARVESTTIME

The Baker's Dozen

WHEN the grasshopper summer was over, some rains came. Some of the sad-looking plants put out new leaves and tried to grow. It was too late for the corn to make new ears or the bean vines to grow more beans.

"How lucky that we have plenty of rutabagas!" said Mr. Glossbrenner cheerfully.

Rutabagas are vegetables which grow in the ground in Minnesota. They are something like beets and something like turnips.

"The grasshoppers did not get many of our potatoes, either," said Mrs. Glossbrenner.

All day long Mr. Glossbrenner and the boys worked to harvest their rutabagas and their potatoes and the wild hay which the grasshoppers had left for them.

At night they counted up their harvest.

Every day Sarah Samantha went out and counted the apples on her tree. It was not hard for her to count them after the grasshoppers were gone. There were thirteen whole apples and fourteen parts of apples left.

Sarah Samantha picked off the parts of apples, and Mrs. Glossbrenner made a small apple pie with them. The apples were small and green, but the pie had a wonderful taste.

"These are good cooking apples," said Mrs.

Glossbrenner. "They will make fine apple dumplings!"

Sarah Samantha wrote to Uncle Romeo. She told him how well the apples were growing. She told him he must be sure to come out to Minnesota this fall.

"And do not forget the lion's tooth!" she said.

On a homestead there were many things to be afraid of, and a lion's tooth was an important thing.

The thirteen apples on the tree grew larger and turned red as autumn came.

"I think they are Winesap apples," said Sarah Samantha's father. "Winesap apples are the finest in the world!"

Sometimes travelers went by the Glossbrenner homestead. They all noticed Miss Appleseed and her thirteen red apples. Most of them wished to buy the apples. Many of them wanted to buy Miss Appleseed.

Sarah Samantha always shook her head hard and said "No."

Mrs. Rollvag and the Apples

ONE DAY Mr. Rollvag came driving out to the homestead with his wife. Mr. Rollvag lived in Deerhorn and owned the store. At harvest-time he drove around to the different home-steads, buying things for his store.

Mrs. Rollvag was a large woman with a loud, bossy voice. She did most of the talking while other people listened.

Mrs. Rollvag reminded Sarah Samantha of Mrs. Perkins, the old lady who had bought her quilted petticoat.

While Mr. Rollvag walked over the fields and around the barnyard with Mr. Gloss-brenner, his wife stayed in the house looking around for more things to buy.

"Do you have eggs to sell?" she asked. "Do you have butter? Do you have any plum preserves or pickled rutabagas? How would you like to sell those blue blankets from the bed? Do you want to get rid of some dishes?"

Suddenly Mrs. Rollvag's sharp, hunting eyes saw Miss Appleseed outside the bedroom window!

Her sharp eyes grew sharper. Her loud voice grew louder.

"Apples!" cried Mrs. Rollvag. "Ripe red apples!"

"That apple tree came all the way from Ohio," said Mrs. Glossbrenner proudly. "They are Winesap apples."

"I will take them all!" said Mrs. Rollvag grandly. "These are the first apples I have seen growing in Minnesota."

"Those apples are not for sale," said Sarah Samantha.

Her parents had always told her that children should be seen and not heard, but this was a special time.

Mrs. Rollvag got up and reached for her basket. "I had better get the apples at once," she said. "I would not want to forget them. They will make a fine apple cake for Sunday supper."

Sarah Samantha said, "No! That is my apple tree. I do not want to sell the apples!"

"Of course I will pay you well for the apples," said Mrs. Rollvag, paying no attention to Sarah Samantha. She added kindly, "I will leave the apple tree, too, of course!"

Sarah Samantha ran after Mrs. Rollvag, who was going out the door. She said in a very loud voice, "I do not want to sell the apples!"

Mrs. Rollvag looked down at Sarah Samantha. She seemed cross. "I will trade you some candy for the apples — a large sack of candy. There will be red and white peppermint sticks. There will be licorice. There will be sourdrops. We have fine candy at the store."

"Candy! Candy!" screamed Annie, who dearly loved all sorts of candy.

Sarah Samantha kept running. She kept saying "No!"

Mrs. Rollvag kept going toward the apple tree. "I will trade you a nice calico dress for the apples," she said. "I have pretty yellow calico with black roses on it. You need a new dress. That one you have on is much too small."

Sarah Samantha ran ahead of Mrs. Rollvag and stood in front of the apple tree. She saw that the large lady was getting very angry. She felt frightened.

Mrs. Rollvag said, "I will give you twenty-five cents each for these silly little apples. But I am in a hurry. You may help me pick the apples, and then I must go!"

Sarah Samantha was almost too frightened to speak. Mrs. Rollvag was even more bossy than Mrs. Perkins.

"You will be a rich little girl when you sell these apples to me!" said Mrs. Rollvag, getting ready to pick an apple. "You will have more than three dollars!"

Sarah Samantha could see her mother and her sisters looking out. Even they were frightened of Mrs. Rollvag and her loud voice and bossy ways. They would not come out and help.

Sarah Samantha stamped her foot on the ground. She held to the apple which the large lady was going to pick.

"I do not want three dollars!" she cried in her loudest voice. "I do not want to sell these apples!"

She held tight to the apple which Mrs. Rollvag was going to pick. The apple came off of the tree, but Sarah Samantha still held on to it.

Mrs. Rollvag took her empty basket and went back to the house. She was very, very angry. Mrs. Glossbrenner offered to sell her a feather pillow and some dried plums, but the lady was too angry to buy anything.

"I am afraid you have made Mrs. Rollvag very cross," said Sarah Samantha's mother when the storekeeper and his wife had driven away.

Miney looked at Sarah Samantha in a surprised way. "Oh, Sarah, how could you?" she cried. "Mrs. Rollvag is so big. Her voice is so loud. She is so stubborn. I would have been scared."

"I was scared!" said Sarah Samantha. Tears rolled down her cheeks as she remembered how scared she had been. "I do not like to be scared," she sobbed. "That is why I had to keep the apples!"

The Moonlight Race

Now there were twelve red apples hanging on the tree. Each day they seemed to grow more beautiful.

Each day somebody in her family asked Sarah Samantha, "When are you going to pick your apples?"

Each day Sarah Samantha answered, "Perhaps I will pick them tomorrow."

She wanted to leave them on the tree as long as she could. The longer they hung on the tree, the bigger and redder they would be.

The nights began to be cool. The moon was very big and bright. When Sarah Samantha went to bed, she could look out the window and see Miss Appleseed standing there in the moonlight, holding her twelve red apples.

"We will have frost before long," Mr. Glossbrenner said one bright moonlight evening.

"Tomorrow I will pick my apples and put them away in a safe place," promised Sarah Samantha.

That night something awakened Sarah Samantha. It was a strange sound. She did not know what made it.

Sarah Samantha opened her eyes. The moon was round and bright in the sky, like a giant's silver dollar. Light from the moon came into the bedroom.

Light from the moon shone over the outdoors. It shone on Miss Appleseed.

Then Sarah Samantha saw what was making the strange sound which had awakened her.

A hungry old pig was eating the apples from the tree! The pig had run away from some other homestead, and he had smelled the apples growing on Sarah Samantha's tree.

He was standing on his back legs, with his

front feet on Miss Appleseed's fence. He was munching and crunching the juicy apples. Apple juice dripped from his jaws to the ground.

Sarah Samantha put on her shoes in a hurry and ran outdoors. The broom was standing by the back door. She took the broom in both hands and hurried around the house.

The pig was just reaching for another apple. He was sniffing and grunting in a hungry way.

If Sarah Samantha had not been in such a hurry, she would have been frightened of the hungry, greedy old pig.

But she had no time to be frightened now. The pig was looking for the biggest and finest apple. He was getting ready to bite it off.

Sarah Samantha came round the house like a windstorm. Whack! Bang! The broom came down hard against the old pig's back legs.

He was surprised. But he kept on reaching for the biggest, reddest apple.

Sarah Samantha cried "Drop that!" in her

loudest, crossest voice, but the pig kept on holding the apple.

Sarah Samantha whacked him hard, first on his back legs and then on his front legs. He climbed down. He looked at Sarah Samantha in a surprised way out of his little black eyes. He backed off. But he still held the biggest, reddest apple in his mouth.

"Let go of that apple!" screamed Sarah Samantha in her most terrible-sounding voice.

She banged the old pig on his ears with the broom. But pigs are tough and not easily hurt by a broom.

The old pig turned around and began to run. Sarah Samantha ran after him, banging him with the broom and crying, "Drop that apple!" as loud as she could.

The loud sounds awakened the rest of the family.

The boys looked out of their window and called sleepily, "What are you doing, Sarah Samantha?"

Mr. and Mrs. Glossbrenner got up and looked out the window into the bright moonlight.

"Where on earth is Sarah Samantha going?" asked Mrs. Glossbrenner.

Mr. Glossbrenner looked out the window into the bright moonlight. He was surprised at what he saw, and hardly knew what to say.

"Who knows?" he answered. "First you would need to know where that pig is going!"

Miney and Annie looked out the window at the middle sister chasing a big, strange old pig in the moonlight.

"Sarah Samantha, come back!" called Miney. "This is not the time to run races and play games with pigs!"

Sarah Samantha heard the voices of her family, but she did not take time to answer. She was too busy running after the pig and trying to make him drop the apple he held in his mouth.

The pig kept running and running. He was

tired of holding a big apple in his mouth, and he was tired of running.

But he could not chew up an apple and swallow it while he was running, and he did not know how to let go of the apple. So he just kept running with the apple in his mouth, and Sarah Samantha ran close behind him banging away with the broom.

They ran for quite a long way across the prairie. Suddenly Sarah Samantha caught her toe on a gopher hole and fell down.

The old pig stopped to rest and take a deep breath. The apple fell out of his mouth and rolled along the ground.

Before he had time to pick it up again, Sarah Samantha had beaten him to it. She picked up the big red apple and wiped it off on her nightgown. The apple was still bright and red, with hardly a mark on it, because the old pig had not had time to bite into it.

"By the time this apple is washed and peeled and made into a dumpling, nobody can tell that an old pig tried to steal it," she thought.

She threw the broom after the pig. "Get on out!" she called.

The pig was glad enough to go on and be away from Sarah Samantha and her loud voice and her broom that banged his legs.

He trotted away in the moonlight, grunting and swinging his head back and forth, and shaking his tiny little tail.

Sarah Samantha sat on the gopher hill, resting. The moon was very bright and round in the sky, and it made the trees and bushes and gopher hills look black.

"My, what a long way I have come!" thought Sarah Samantha. She looked all around. The barn and the house seemed far away. "Of course, they are not so far as they seem," said Sarah Samantha to herself. "This prairie is not so big as it seems, either."

She listened. The moonlight seemed filled with strange sounds. It seemed to her that she could hear the sound of somebody crying.

"I am not really as scared as I think I am," said Sarah Samantha to herself.

Sarah Samantha's Indian

SARAH SAMANTHA listened awhile longer. The more she listened, the more strange and wild and lonely the night sounds seemed.

The strangest and most lonely sound came from some bushes a little distance ahead of Sarah Samantha.

"That sounds like Annie when she has been spanked or has a stomach-ache or is frightened of something!" thought Sarah Samantha, listening.

The noise behind the bushes was a sort of whining and crying and sobbing.

"Of course it is not Annie!" laughed Sarah Samantha to herself in the moonlight. "Annie is safe at home in her bed!" She rubbed and polished the apple again. "I had better be going home now," she said. "I got the apple away from that old pig. I must go home and finish my sleep!"

The whining behind the bushes seemed louder.

"It could be a lost dog," thought Sarah Samantha. "It could be a little puppy which is lost from its mother!"

She looked closely toward the bushes. In the bright moonlight the bushes looked like spots of black ink.

When she looked very, very closely she could see another black spot under the bushes. The strange, lonely sound was coming from the other black spot.

"If I only had my lion's tooth, I would not be afraid to go over there and look under those bushes!" said Sarah Samantha.

Something moved under the bushes. Sarah Samantha was more afraid than ever, but she went over and looked under the bushes.

A little tiny boy was sitting there. His hair was long and black. His face was dark. He was a little Indian boy who had become lost from his people.

When he saw Sarah Samantha looking down at him, he whined softly, like a little frightened puppy.

Indians do not cry easily, but this was a very small, very young Indian.

Sarah Samantha had always been afraid of Indians. Back in Ohio there were no Indians, but sometimes, out here in Minnesota, Indians would walk or ride past the homesteads.

Sarah Samantha had tried never to look at the Minnesota Indians. They had such sharp eyes and such black hair and such dark skins. Their voices had a strange, wild sound.

Sarah Samantha's brothers liked to read stories about Indians, and they liked to tell the stories to Sarah Samantha because it was fun to see her look frightened.

Sarah Samantha had never expected to

meet any Indians, not even after she got her lion's tooth.

The little Indian boy looked up at Sarah Samantha standing there in her white night-gown with a red apple in her hand.

He said, in a little scared voice, "Lost! Hungry!"

Then Sarah Samantha did not feel so much afraid of him. She put out her hands and helped him stand up.

"Come with me!" she said. "We will find the way home together!"

Then Sarah Samantha and the little Indian walked back home, hand in hand. It took much longer to go back than it had taken Sarah Samantha to come.

At last they reached the house. All the family came running through the moonlight to meet them. The little Indian was frightened. He whined and hung tight to Sarah Samantha's hand.

The family could hardly believe what they

saw. For once, even Miney could think of nothing to say. The boys looked at each other in surprise.

"Sarah Samantha has caught an Indian!" whispered Robert to Silas.

Silas whispered back, "All by herself, our sister Sarah Samantha has gone out at night and captured an Indian!"

Mrs. Glossbrenner picked up the little Indian in her arms. "He is only a baby," she said, "only a little lost baby!"

They took the little Indian into the house. He was very tired and dirty and hungry. Mrs. Glossbrenner washed his face and hands. Mr. Glossbrenner brought him some bread and milk from the cupboard. Miney found some clean clothes for him to wear. The boys stirred the fire in the iron cookstove so he could warm his feet.

The little Indian boy stopped whining. He looked at the family, and his eyes were dark and frightened. Two tears rolled down his dark cheeks. Sarah Samantha felt sorry for the homesick, lonely child.

All the family tried to make the little Indian smile, but he would not smile.

Then Sarah Samantha had an idea. She took the big red apple which the old pig had tried to steal. She laid it in the little boy's brown hands.

Then a very large smile came slowly on the little boy's face. He looked at the apple and smiled. He smelled it, and laughed. He bit into the red apple, and juice ran down his chin.

"Good! Good!" he said.

Miney yawned. "This has been an exciting night, and I am tired," she said. "It is not every night that Sarah Samantha runs after a pig and catches an Indian."

The moon was getting pale now. Most of the night was gone.

"We must all go back to bed," said Mrs. Glossbrenner after she had made a nice bed of blankets for the little Indian.

"First I have some work to do," said Sarah Samantha.

She took a basket from the shelf and went out to the apple tree. There were eight apples left on the tree, and she picked each apple carefully and put it in the basket.

"Now I can go to sleep," she said, coming back into the house.

She put the basket of apples under her bed.

"Now the apple harvest is over," she said. "I will not need to worry about the frost or the wild pigs. I must write to Uncle Romeo and let him know that the apples are ready."

Little Buffalo

THE SMALL INDIAN stayed for several days with the Glossbrenner family. He got over being scared, and grew quite friendly and cheerful. His name was Little Buffalo.

"We must get word to his people," said Mr. Glossbrenner. "They will be looking for him."

He rode to Deerhorn and left word at Mr. Rollvag's store. "Tell everybody that the lost Indian child is at my homestead," he said.

Indians came from miles around to do their trading at Deerhorn.

Little Buffalo could not say a great many words. He knew "hungry," "cold," "bread," "good," "horse," and other easy words.

He had learned a new word the night he came home with Sarah Samantha. That word was "apple." Over and over again he would say "apple." He would smile when he said it. He would pretend to be biting into a juicy, ripe red apple.

Miney taught him to say "Please" for things he wanted.

Then he would say, "Apple please please apple!" over and over and over.

But Sarah Samantha did not give him any more apples. She had hidden the apples away very carefully, and she had not told anybody where they were.

They were in a basket away up in the attic not far from the chimney. There they would not get too hot and dry up. There they would not freeze when the winter came.

She had written to Uncle Romeo, and Mr. Glossbrenner had mailed the letter at Deerhorn. Her brothers laughed at Sarah Samantha.

"How silly to think that Uncle Romeo will

come all the way from Ohio to Minnesota just for an apple dumpling!" they said often.

Miney often said, "It is too bad to waste those good red apples. You might as well let Mother make an apple pie for us. Or we could eat the apples before they spoil."

But Sarah Samantha shook her head.

Even when Little Buffalo held out his hands and said "Apple please please apple good apple please!" she kept on shaking her head.

The frost came and the wild geese flew south again. Still Uncle Romeo did not come from Ohio, and still Little Buffalo stayed on with the Glossbrenner family.

He was fat and cheerful now. He laughed and played with Annie, who was about his size. He learned to wash his face and hands and to say "Thank you!"

"He is like a little brother to us," said Sarah Samantha. "I have always wished for a small, young brother!"

One day Mrs. Glossbrenner looked out the

doorway. She saw something which frightened her. She saw a great many Indians coming. She tried to act brave.

"Do not be afraid," she said to the children. "I am sure these are friendly Indians. We will be friendly to them and give them food."

Little Buffalo saw the Indians. He began to laugh and clap his hands. He was not afraid, because these were his people.

The Indians came riding into the yard on their ponies. There were several Indian men and women. An old Indian man rode in front. He got down first and came to the door.

Mrs. Glossbrenner opened the door. "Welcome!" she said in a trembling voice.

The old Indian man said, "Hi!"

He came into the house, and the other Indians followed him.

They said, "Hi!"

Little Buffalo came running from behind the door. He ran to the old Indian, and the old Indian picked him up in his arms.

"Hi, Grandfather!" said Little Buffalo.

The old Indian said, "Hi, Grandson!"

All the other Indians smiled and said, "Hi, Little Buffalo!"

Then Mrs. Glossbrenner and her daughters got very busy. Mrs. Glossbrenner boiled a great kettle of potatoes. She put meat on to fry. She baked many large pans of corn bread.

When Mr. Glossbrenner and the boys came in from their woodcutting at noon, they were surprised to see that they had company.

Miney had been telling the Indians how Sarah Samantha saved Little Buffalo. She had told them over and over.

When she finished telling them, the Indians laughed and clapped their hands. "Tell more!" they said.

So Miney had talked until she was tired of talking. "You tell," she said to Sarah Samantha.

But Sarah Samantha was too scared to talk. Her knees shook when she walked. Her hands shook when she got out the dishes. Her voice was small and weak when she spoke, and it shook too.

When the Indians looked at her and cried "Good girl!" she wanted to run and hide.

Little Buffalo's people enjoyed the meal with the Glossbrenner family. They ate in a hungry way. They ate everything on the table. They ate the potatoes. They ate the corn bread. They ate the meat and the boiled beans. They drank all the milk.

They sat there, smiling and looking hungry and waiting for more.

Mrs. Glossbrenner quickly made some more kettles of mush, and the visitors ate that. They ate pickled rutabagas and some raw turnips.

When there was nothing left to eat, they sat there smiling and waiting.

Little Buffalo said, "Apple! Please apple!"

Sarah Samantha shook her head. "There is nothing left!" she said. "That is all!"

Then the Indians got up.

Big Buffalo took Little Buffalo in his arms.

"We go now!" he said.

Big Buffalo came over to Sarah Samantha. He looked at her out of his black eyes, and Sarah Samantha felt like running and hiding, because she was such a timid girl.

But the Indian grandfather spoke kindly. "You are brave!" he said. "I call you Buffalo Woman!"

Then the Indians rode out of the yard. Big Buffalo rode ahead with Little Buffalo hanging on.

"Good-by, Little Buffalo!" the Glossbrenners called, waving their hands. "Come back and see us again!"

Little Buffalo waved back. "Good-by thank you!" he called, smiling because he knew so many words.

THE APPLE DUMPLING

The Great Day

WINTER came again. The snow fell thick and white about the homestead.

But the Glossbrenners were used to the Minnesota winters now. The weather did not seem so cold. The sounds did not seem so wild and lonely.

Mr. Glossbrenner and the boys piled wood in great heaps behind the house. There was plenty of wood to keep the stoves burning day and night.

Sarah Samantha brought wild hay from the barn and packed it around Miss Appleseed's roots. She got the old horse blanket and tied it about the tree's branches.

She could hardly reach the top of the tree now. Soon Miss Appleseed would be too big for her picket fence and her horse-blanket shawl!

Sarah Samantha watched carefully after the basket of apples. She did not allow them to get too cold and freeze. She did not allow them to get too warm and dry up.

One day Mr. Glossbrenner got an exciting letter at Deerhorn. The letter was from Uncle Romeo.

"I am coming to Minnesota to visit you," wrote Uncle Romeo. "Who knows? I may even stay. In a fast-growing state like Minnesota there will soon be a circus which will need good men to work for it!"

The family could hardly wait for the day when Uncle Romeo would arrive. Mr. Glossbrenner and the boys hurried to build a new room on one side of the house for Uncle Romeo.

Mrs. Glossbrenner and the girls planned all the good things they could have to eat when their favorite uncle came.

"And at last I can make my apple dumpling!" said Sarah Samantha.

She thought, "I do hope Uncle Romeo will not forget the lion's tooth!"

Every day she looked at the apples to see that they were all right. Every day she sang a song which Miney had made up for her.

It was a song which told how to make apple dumplings:

> What are apple dumplings made of?
> What are apple dumplings made of?
>   Sugar and spice,
>   And apples so nice.
> That's what apple dumplings are made of!

The song had several verses, but Sarah Samantha liked best the verse about the sugar and spice.

At last the great day came when Uncle Romeo would arrive at Deerhorn.

Uncle Romeo would come on the train from Ohio. Mr. Glossbrenner would meet him at Deerhorn with the horses and wagon.

"Who wants to go with me to meet Uncle Romeo?" he asked.

"I do!" said the boys together.

"I do!" said Annie and Miney together.

"I would like to go with you to meet Uncle Romeo!" said Mrs. Glossbrenner.

Only Sarah Samantha did not want to go. "I will stay here and make my apple dumpling," she said.

All the family looked at her in surprise.

"You will stay here—alone—all by yourself?"

Sarah Samantha nodded her head. "I will be busy," she said. "I will be making my apple dumpling. It will take me a good while, because I must be very careful!"

The rest of the family got into the wagon and drove off toward Deerhorn.

Sarah Samantha stirred the fire in the black iron cookstove. She looked into the big, square oven. It was nice and warm.

She got out the pans and spoons and the rolling pin. She got out a knife to peel the apples.

She sang as she worked.

What are apple dumplings made of?
What are apple dumplings made of?
　Sugar and spice,
　Everything nice.
　Sugar and spice,
　Everything nice.
　Sugar and spice,
　Everything nice!

Over and over she sang her favorite lines.
"Sugar and spice have such a pleasant
sound!" she thought.

Sugar 'n' Spice

SARAH SAMANTHA climbed up to the attic where the basket of apples was hidden against the chimney.

She brought the basket downstairs and took the apples out.

"How beautiful you are!" she said. "How good you smell! What a fine apple dumpling you will make for Uncle Romeo!"

She set the eight red apples in a row on the table, where she could look at them.

"I might as well get my dough ready," she thought. "It is better to be too early than too late!"

She got out the flour and the fat and the milk. And she got out the little cans of spice. She stood on tiptoe and reached up for the sugar jar.

The sugar jar was empty! There was not a spoonful of sugar in it!

Then Sarah Samantha remembered. The sugar jar had been empty for several days. Her father and mother had been using molasses in their coffee all week. The children had been eating molasses on their mush for several days.

"You can make a fine cake with molasses," her mother had said only yesterday.

Sarah Samantha felt like crying. But she had no time to cry.

"I must think about my apple dumplings!" she said. "An apple dumpling needs sugar."

She looked out the back door. The homestead looked very big.

"Mrs. MacDonald would have sugar," she thought. "She would let me borrow some sugar for my dumpling."

It seemed a very long way to the MacDonald homestead. It seemed so much longer when she was alone.

Sarah Samantha kept walking. She tried not to see how big the prairie seemed or how small she felt. She walked as fast as she could.

"Soon I will not be afraid of anything!" she thought to herself when she heard a strange sound or saw a big gopher looking out of his hole at her.

Mrs. MacDonald was surprised to see Sarah Samantha all by herself. She begged Sarah Samantha to stay with her and visit.

"Mr. MacDonald has gone over to another homestead to talk about building a school-house," she said. "Stay with me till he comes home, and then he will take you back on his horse."

Sarah Samantha shook her head. "I must be getting home with my sugar," she said. "It takes a long time to make an apple dumpling that will be good enough for Uncle Romeo."

So Mrs. MacDonald gave her some sugar wrapped up in a white cloth.

"Be very careful going back home alone," she said, speaking in a worried voice because she was such a timid woman.

Sarah Samantha walked home as fast as she could. Over and over as she walked she sang the song about the apple dumpling. She sang all the verses. Then she began all over and sang her favorite verse:

> What are apple dumplings made of?
> What are apple dumplings made of?
>   Sugar 'n' spice,
>   Sugar 'n' spice,
>   Sugar 'n' spice . . .
> That's what apple dumplings are made of!

And Then There Was One

AT LAST Sarah Samantha got back home. When she came to her house, she saw something which made her stop still and look.

Two spotted ponies were standing in front of the house. They were Indian ponies.

Sarah Samantha's knees felt shaky. Her heart beat very fast and loud. She went up and looked in through the kitchen window. What she saw made her feel like running away.

There at the table sat two Indians. One was a very large old Indian, and one was a very small young Indian.

They were sitting by the table where Sarah Samantha's eight red apples had been laid out ready to go into an apple dumpling.

Where were the eight apples?

Sarah Samantha looked more closely. She saw one apple left. It was the runt apple — the smallest of them all.

While she watched, the big old Indian reached out his brown hand and picked up the apple. He opened his mouth, ready to bite the apple in two with his big teeth.

Then Sarah Samantha opened the door. She came in very fast. She got in just in time to get the apple before it went into the Indian's mouth!

"Hi!" said the Indians.

Sarah Samantha looked more closely at them. It was Big Buffalo and Little Buffalo. They smiled at her in a friendly way.

"Where are my apples?" asked Sarah Samantha.

The Indians smiled again.

Little Buffalo said, "Apple! Good!"

Big Buffalo said, "All good! All gone!"

He pointed to the little apple which Sarah Samantha had taken from him. "One for you too!" he said kindly.

Sarah Samantha felt like crying. But there was no use in crying over apples which were already eaten!

She looked at the apple in her hand. It was a very small apple. But it was a real apple, and she had picked it herself from Miss Appleseed.

Sarah Samantha tied on her apron. She washed her hands. She stirred the fire in the black iron cookstove.

Then she spoke in a stern voice to the Indians. "Do not bother me now. I have important work to do. I must make an apple dumpling for Uncle Romeo!"

She mixed the dough for the dumpling and rolled it out. Then she peeled the one apple. It was a very small apple. It looked even smaller when it was cut in pieces and piled in the middle of the big piece of dough.

Sarah Samantha put in lots of sugar. She put in lots of spice. She rolled up the apple dumpling and put it in the oven to bake.

Big Buffalo and Little Buffalo watched her as she worked. They were very quiet and did not bother her. Now and then they smiled at each other in a proud way.

Every minute or two Sarah Samantha opened the oven door and looked in at the apple dumpling. It seemed to her that it was baking very slowly.

"The fire is too low!" she said. "Bring wood quickly. Make the fire hot!"

Big Buffalo and Little Buffalo went out and got wood. They built up the kitchen fire for Sarah Samantha. They did not stop to talk.

"How surprised all the people back in Ohio would be to see Indians helping me with my apple dumpling!" thought Sarah Samantha.

She did not have time to feel frightened at the strange thought.

The Present

At last the apple dumpling was done. Sarah Samantha took it out of the oven. It was brown and hot. It had a sweet smell of sugar and spice and apple.

Big Buffalo and Little Buffalo looked at the dumpling in a hungry way.

"Good! Good!" they said together.

Big Buffalo smiled. "Hungry. Very hungry!" he said. He held out his hands to the apple dumpling.

Sarah Samantha shook her head. She carried the apple dumpling into her bedroom and hid it under the bed.

Then she came back to the kitchen. She got bread and molasses for Big Buffalo and Little Buffalo. The Indians enjoyed the good food. They ate several loaves of bread and a jug of molasses.

Then Big Buffalo stood up. He smiled at Sarah Samantha. "We go now," he said. Then he took Sarah Samantha by her hand. "Come!" he said.

Sarah Samantha was too frightened to answer. She went with Big Buffalo to the front yard, where the spotted ponies were standing.

Then the big old Indian said, "You are a brave girl. Your name is Buffalo Woman. We have brought a present for Buffalo Woman who saved Little Buffalo!"

He pointed to one of the spotted ponies which was tied to a post in the front yard.

"For you!" he said to Sarah Samantha. "He rides like the wind. He will take you fast everywhere. His name is Lightning!"

Lightning, the pony, had wild eyes and

shaggy hair. He looked at Sarah Samantha out of his wild eyes and sprang into the air, waving his front feet and his tail.

Then Big Buffalo jumped to the back of the other pony. He lifted Little Buffalo in front of him.

"Good-by, good-by!" called the Indians.

Big Buffalo waved his hand. "Good-by, Buffalo Woman," called Big Buffalo. "We will come back to see you ride on Lightning someday!"

The Lion's Tooth

Before long, Sarah Samantha heard the sound of the wagon coming. She rushed out to meet Uncle Romeo.

Uncle Romeo was as handsome as ever. He was as full of jokes as he had always been. He pretended to be afraid of Sarah Samantha.

"Who is this great big tall person?" he asked. "Surely this is not little Sarah Samantha?"

While Mrs. Glossbrenner and Miney were putting supper on the table, Sarah Samantha and Uncle Romeo hurried out to look at Miss Appleseed. Uncle Romeo was surprised.

"Surely this great, tall apple tree cannot be little Miss Appleseed!" he said. Then he looked at Lightning, the spotted Indian pony. "Who rides this wild, dangerous-acting creature?" he asked.

Sarah Samantha answered, "He is my pony. I shall ride him when he is older and I am braver!"

The family sat down to supper. It was a good supper, and the table was well filled with food which Mrs. Glossbrenner had cooked.

Finally Sarah Samantha got up from the table. She went into the bedroom and reached under the bed. The apple dumpling was still there, covered up with a towel.

It was a proud moment for the middle sister. She set the apple dumpling down in front of Uncle Romeo.

Her voice shook when she spoke. "Here is an apple dumpling. I baked it for you all by myself, from an apple that grew on Miss Appleseed. I have kept our bargain!"

Then Uncle Romeo reached into his pocket. He got out the lion's tooth with the gold chain on it. The lion's tooth was just as white and shiny as ever. The chain was as long and bright as ever.

Uncle Romeo put the chain around Sarah Samantha's neck and fastened it. "The lion's tooth is yours now!" he said. "You have earned it with this good apple dumpling!"

The Charm That Worked

Sᴀʀᴀʜ Sᴀᴍᴀɴᴛʜᴀ ran outdoors. She looked all about her, hunting for things to be afraid of.

She hurried out to the barn where the pigs were walking about in a sleepy way.

"I am not afraid of you any more!" she called to the pigs.

She went into the henhouse. She did not feel afraid of the scolding hens.

She went out to the barn, looking here and there in the granary and up in the barn loft and under old boards for rats to be afraid of. She was disappointed because all the rats were hiding and would not come out.

Old Susie, the cross cow, shook her head at Sarah Samantha and mooed at her in a disagreeable voice.

"You are not dangerous!" Sarah Samantha called to her.

Finally she went back to the house. She had hunted everywhere for dangerous things and she did not feel afraid of anything.

"Uncle Romeo was right!" she thought happily. "A person who wears a lion's tooth is as brave as a lion. I am as brave as a lion!"

She ran around to the post where Lightning, the spotted Indian pony, was standing. He stamped his foot and tossed his head in a wild way. He made a loud sound with his nose.

Sarah Samantha looked at him for quite a while. She tried to think how it would be to ride on his back across the prairies. She felt glad that he was only a colt, and was not old enough to ride yet.

"It is a lucky thing that I have a lion's tooth!" said Sarah Samantha to the spotted Indian pony.